JACK

THE GIANT CHASER

AN APPALACHIAN TALE

KENN & JOANNE COMPTON

HOLIDAY HOUSE • NEW YORK

For our grandparents—
Pink and Della
Ernest and Annie
Montgomery and Verbie
Julian and Josephine

Text copyright © 1993 by Kenn and Joanne Compton
Illustrations copyright © 1993 by Kenn Compton
ALL RIGHTS RESERVED
Printed in the United States of America
FIRST EDITION

Library of Congress Cataloging-in-Publication Data
Compton, Kenn.
    Jack the giant chaser : an Appalachian tale /
Kenn and Joanne Compton.
        p.   cm.
    Summary: Jack uses his wits to get rid of the giant
up on Balsam Mountain.
    ISBN 0-8234-0998-8
    [1. Folklore—United States.   2. Giants—Folklore.]   I. Compton,
Joanne.   II. Title.
PZ8.1.C7356Jac   1993   92-15911   CIP   AC
398.21—dc20
[E]

A NOTE FROM THE AUTHORS

We grew up listening to our parents, grandparents, and great aunts and uncles as they told old stories, jokes, and family anecdotes. Joanne lived in eastern North Carolina and was fascinated by Uncle Remus tales and ghost stories. Kenn grew up in the mountains of western North Carolina, and his favorites were the Southern Appalachian Jack Tales. *Jack the Giant Chaser* is a retelling of one of those stories.

Many of the Jack Tales have elements common to the fairy tales collected by Jacobs and Grimm, but, as they were passed from generation to generation, they were shaped by the culture of their American storytellers. Our version of *Jack the Giant Chaser* is adapted from Richard Chase's *Jack and the Giants' Newground*, found in the volume *The Jack Tales*, published by Houghton Mifflin Co. in 1943. In the original story, Jack is sent by the king to get rid of a family of five giants; we focus instead on Jack's confrontation with just one giant.

Joanne and Kenn Compton
April 1992

One sunny day, Jack was returning home after running off some highway robbers. As he ambled down the road by the creek, minding his own business, he spied seven catfish swimming along the bank. Jack was feeling hungry, so he leaned over, picked up a smooth rock, and heaved it at those catfish. Wouldn't you know, one rock hit all seven and killed 'em dead! Jack cleaned 'em, cooked 'em, and had himself a fine dinner.

After he'd eaten, Jack traveled on and traveled on until he came to his hometown. There, he noticed most of his neighbors and kinfolk were gathered in front of the general store. Jack walked up to them and announced, "I'm back." Nobody paid any attention. So he said, just a little bit louder this time, "Yep, I just had me a fine adventure." When the townsfolk continued to ignore him, Jack hollered, "I just killed me seven with one blow!"

Well, that got folks' attention! Suddenly everybody crowded around Jack. "Seven with one blow!" they exclaimed. The townspeople made such a fuss that Jack didn't have the heart to tell them it was only seven catfish that he'd killed.

Finally the mayor got everybody to quiet down so he could make a speech. He called Jack up to the steps of the store and said, "Jack, since you been gone we've had nothing but trouble. Seems this mean old giant has taken to living up on Balsam Mountain. And he don't take too kindly to us down here."

"Last week he come off the mountain and stole three of my best milk cows!" shouted Old Man Ward.

"He stomped my whole field of corn and ruined half the rhubarb, too!" yelled Cousin Harmon.

"You oughta see how he pushed over my barn!" exclaimed Miss Josephine. "None of us has had any peace for weeks!"

The mayor hooked his arm around Jack's shoulders and declared, "What we need is a giant chaser, and I believe you are just the one for the job."

With that, Jack's neighbors and kinfolk hooped and hollered and slapped poor old Jack on the back. Jack wasn't so sure he was cut out to deal with giants. But since everybody thought he was a hero, he figured he'd have to try and act like one.

The next morning, Jack got up bright and early and set off to Balsam Mountain to find that giant. When he got up there, the giant wasn't home so Jack set himself down bold as you please on the front porch to wait for him. Wasn't long before the giant appeared over the ridge, carrying Miss Palmer's two prize pigs, one in each hand.

"Howdy," said Jack.

"Howdy, yourself," replied the giant as he set down the pigs. "What you doing setting on my front porch, little man?"

"I'm hunting a giant. You seen one around here?"

"Haw! Seen one? Don't you know I *am* one?"

Jack looked that giant over and said,
"I dunno. Most of the giants I've
seen are lots bigger than you.
But I reckon you're the one
I'm aiming to get rid of."

The giant just busted out laughing. "What makes you think you'z a match for me, little fellow?"

Jack looked surprised. "Why, I figured you'd heard of me. I'm Jack, and just yesterday I killed seven with one blow."

"Seven! Is that a fact?" The giant looked surprised.

"Yep," said Jack. "Seven. Of course, I'm kinda the small one in my family. If my daddy was to catch up with you, I'd hate to think what'd happen."

"Well," said the giant, "you must be tougher than you look, Jack. Before we commence to fighting, how'd you like to have something to eat?"

"Why, that's right neighborly," said Jack. "I reckon I can wait until this afternoon to take care of you."

Now that old giant aimed to find out just how tough Jack was. So he went inside and got two huge buckets.

"Let's go down to the creek and fetch up some water to cook with, Jack," said the giant.

Jack knew there was no way he could even pick up the two buckets, much less lug them up the hill, full of water. But he had himself an idea. When they got to the creek, Jack waded out into the middle and reached down to the bottom.

"What you doing there, Jack?" asked the giant.

"I'm a-fixin' to grab hold of the creek so I can drag it up to your front door. No sense carrying just a little bit of water up there."

"Whoa there, Jack! I don't want the creek that close to my house. It might flood me out someday. Just you grab one of these buckets and we'll be done."

"Not me," said Jack. "If I can't carry the creek, I'll not be caught carrying this little bit of water! What if my kinfolk saw me?"

So the giant grabbed up both of those buckets himself and toted them up the hill to the cabin.

After he got dinner started, the giant said to Jack, "Let's go outside and play a little mumblety-peg while the greens are cooking."

"All right by me," said Jack.

They went outside, and the giant pulled out his pocketknife and threw it clear across the yard and straight into the ground. "Your turn, little man," he said to Jack.

Jack walked over to the knife and sized it up. It was nearly as tall as himself and probably weighed 150 pounds. There's no way I can pull this out of the ground much less throw it, Jack was thinking to himself. Didn't take Jack long, though, to come up with an idea.

Looking out across the valley and the far mountains, Jack hollered, "Hey, uncle!"

"Who you calling uncle?" roared the giant. "I ain't your kin!"

"I ain't talking to you. I'm yelling to my uncle who lives on the far side of those mountains. He could use a good knife like this one, so I figured I'd just toss it over to him."

"Hold on there, Jack! That's my good knife, and I'm not ready to part with it. You just toss it right here in the yard."

"Well," said Jack, "if I can't throw it where I please, I won't throw it at all. What if my kin saw me?" And he stomped into the cabin.

The giant went inside, too, and dished up two plates of cornbread, greens, and ham. Then he and Jack sat down to eat.

While they were eating, Jack began cocking his head to one side and glancing out the window. He kept doing it until he started to make the giant kind of nervous.

"What you looking at?" demanded the giant.

"Nothin'," replied Jack. "I'm just looking to see what I can see."

"Well, cut it out!" said the giant. "You're starting to rile me."

They kept on eating, and all the while Jack's eyes were glued to the window. Once, he muttered out of the side of his mouth, "Hee haw! Here they come!"

"What do you see out that window, little man?" growled the giant.

"Oh, it's nothin'," snickered Jack. "But, if I was you, I'd hurry up and finish my dinner."

"Now, hold your horses!" cried the giant. "First you better tell me what you spied out that window."

"Oh, it's nothin', I tell you," laughed Jack. "Nothin' but my daddy, my two big brothers, and about two dozen of my other kinfolk."

Now the giant remembered that Jack said he was the smallest one in his family, and he got this bug-eyed look on his face.

"Land's sake, if all of them catch up with me at once, I'm as good as dead for sure. You gotta hide me, little man!"

Jack looked that giant over and said, "Now why would I wanna do that?"

"Aw, please don't let them catch me. I'll leave this valley, and you'll never see me again!"

"Well, I don't know. You promise you won't be back?"

"Oh, I promise, I promise!"

Jack peered around the room and then told the giant, "Quick, jump into your big ole barrel over in the corner and I'll do what I can to get shed of them."

It took some doing, but after a lot of shoving and squeezing, the giant was finally crammed into the barrel, and Jack slammed the lid on as tightly as he could.

Then Jack began making all kinds of
commotion in the cabin, pretending like
his kinfolk were really there. He turned
over chairs, threw pots and pans around,
and dumped drawers in the floor. All the
while he was hollering and screeching
like twenty men.

Then Jack shook that giant's barrel real hard
and shouted, "He ain't here, I tell you! There
ain't no giants in this cabin!"

Finally Jack rolled the barrel to the door and shoved it off the porch. Jack ran after it as it bounced and bumped all the way down the mountain until — *Smack* — it hit a tree.

Out crawled the giant. "I'm much obliged to you, little man. You saved my life," said the giant, rubbing the bump on his head.

"Oh, it was nothing," Jack told him. "Now you better hightail it out of here 'fore those boys come back lookin' for you."

The giant bolted across the creek, over the ridge, and past the state line.

And that was the last Jack or anybody in those parts ever saw of that bothersome creature.